ELBERT
IN THE AIR

written by
MONICA WESOLOWSKA

illustrated by
JEROME PUMPHREY

Dial Books for Young Readers

Shortly after he was born, Elbert floated into the air.

Soon his mother had to stretch to reach him.

When people heard she stood on tiptoes to feed him, they came from all around to give advice.

"Net him like a butterfly,"
suggested one neighbor.

"Reel him in like a kite,"
urged another.

"Deflate him," insisted a
stranger, "like a balloon."

But Elbert was not a butterfly.
Nor a kite.
Nor a balloon.

Elbert was Elbert, and when he cooed in the air, his mother merely said, "If Elbert was born to float, I will let him."

As Elbert grew, he floated higher.
Soon his mother had to climb the furniture to reach him.

All day long, she tossed him toys, which Elbert used
to build a floating world above her head.
"Look, Ma!" he exclaimed.
"Fantastic, Elbert!" she replied.
And for a while, it was.

But Elbert grew.

And grew.

When he outgrew his toy world, he somersaulted out the window to spend his days playing by himself above the yard.

But one day, he just hovered.

"Even on my birthday," he sighed, "no one else is up here."

"Don't worry," his mother said, climbing a ladder with his cake.

"I'm here. Now make a wish!"

So Elbert did, and while he waited for his wish to come true,
he shared his cake with some squirrels.

The next day, Elbert spotted a group of children starting school.
"Look, Ma!" he called. "I'm ready to join them!"
But when Elbert entered through the classroom window,
his teacher called for help.

"Assign him bigger books,"
recommended the librarian.

"Issue him heavier shoes,"
prescribed the nurse.

"Glue him,"
dictated the secretary,
"to his chair!"

No matter what he tried,
Elbert didn't fit in.

His tears fell like rain.

But when they tried to send him home, Elbert's mother sternly shook her head and said, "If Elbert was born to float, you should let him!"

Elbert soon learned to fold his schoolwork into fancy paper airplanes to land on his teacher's desk.

At recess, he caught the highest balls and tagged
his classmates with his shadow.
"Fantastic, Elbert!" his mother said.

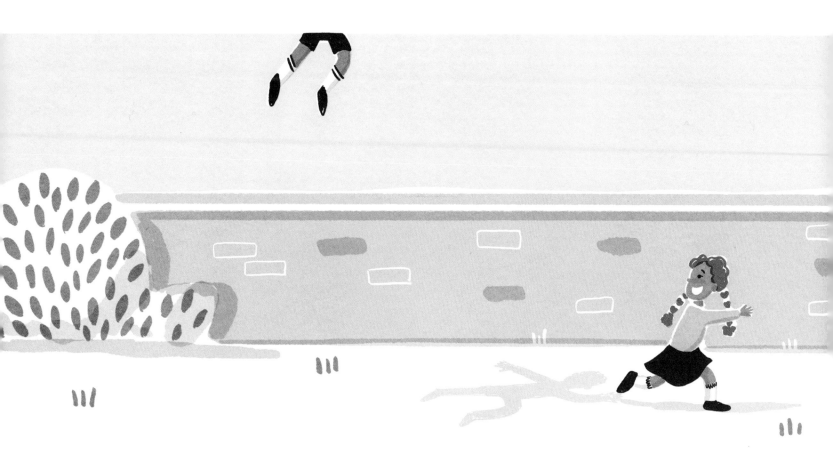

And for a while, it was.

But Elbert grew.

And grew.

And as he grew, his distance from his classmates widened until he couldn't join their games no matter how he tried.

To keep him company one night, his mother climbed a fire escape.
"Just be yourself," she soothed him, "and you'll find friends."
Then she handed him a bowl of popcorn big enough to share.

"Look, Ma!" he cheered, spotting a shooting star.

"Fantastic, Elbert," she replied. "Make a wish."
So Elbert did . . .

The next day, Elbert carried his wish all over town
until a crowd complained he was causing a commotion.

"Anchor him like a boat,"
preached a bus driver.

"Hook him like a fish,"
growled a dog walker.

"Forbid all floating,"
demanded the mayor,
"and arrest him."

Fortunately, Elbert was Elbert.
No hook, no anchor, no law could bring him down!

So when his mother scrambled up a crane to defend him,
he bravely reassured her, "Don't worry, Ma. I'll just float higher!"

But as he rose and everyone shrank, Elbert's heart grew heavy.

Just then something
nudged him.

"Thanks, Ma!" Elbert cried, blowing down a kiss.

High enough
to find . . .

And higher.

And with that,
he floated higher.

. . . the world he'd always wished for!

&,

DEAREST MA,

CLIMB
THIS
ROPE.

And it was fantastic.

For supportive parents everywhere, including my own —MW

For Lily, Ryden, and Effie —JP

Dial Books for Young Readers
An imprint of Penguin Random House LLC, New York

First published in the United States of America by Dial Books for Young Readers,
an imprint of Penguin Random House LLC, 2023

Text copyright © 2023 by Monica Wesolowska
Illustrations copyright © 2023 by Jerome Pumphrey

Dial & colophon are registered trademarks of Penguin Random House LLC.
Visit us online at penguinrandomhouse.com.

Library of Congress Cataloging-in-Publication Data is available.

Manufactured in China • ISBN 9780593325209
TOPL

1 3 5 7 9 10 8 6 4 2

Design by Jenny Kelly • Text set in Futura Com

The art was created digitally and includes textures created with tea-stained paper.